A NOTE TO PARENTS

When your children are ready to "step into reading," giving them the right books—and lots of them—is as crucial as giving them the right food to eat. **Step into Reading Books** present exciting stories and information reinforced with lively, colorful illustrations that make learning to read fun, satisfying, and worthwhile. They are priced so that acquiring an entire library of them is affordable. And they are beginning readers with an important difference—they're written on four levels.

Step 1 Books, with their very large type and extremely simple vocabulary, have been created for the very youngest readers. **Step 2 Books** are both longer and slightly more difficult. **Step 3 Books,** written to mid-second-grade reading levels, are for the child who has acquired even greater reading skills. **Step 4 Books** offer exciting nonfiction for the increasingly proficient reader.

Children develop at different ages. **Step into Reading Books,** with their four levels of reading, are designed to help children become good—and interested—readers *faster*. The grade levels assigned to the four steps—preschool through grade 1 for Step 1, grades 1 through 3 for Step 2, grades 2 and 3 for Step 3, and grades 2 through 4 for Step 4—are intended only as guides. Some children move through all four steps very rapidly; others climb the steps over a period of several years. These books will help your child "step into reading" in style!

Library of Congress Cataloging-in-Publication Data
Hayward, Linda.
The biggest cookie in the world / by Linda Hayward ; illustrated by Joe Ewers.
  p. cm. — (Step into reading. A Step 1 book)
SUMMARY: While waiting for his cookies to bake in the oven, Cookie Monster daydreams about his favorite subject.
ISBN 0-679-87146-2 (trade) — ISBN 0-679-97146-7 (lib. bdg.)
[1. Cookies—Fiction. 2. Baking—Fiction. 3. Monsters—Fiction.]
I. Ewers, Joe, ill. II. Children's Television Workshop. III. Title. IV. Series: Step into reading. Step 1 book.
PZ7.H31495Bi 1995 94-21151 [E]—dc20

Manufactured in the United States of America 10 9 8 7 6 5 4 3 2 1

STEP INTO READING is a trademark of Random House, Inc.

Step into Reading™

THE BIGGEST COOKIE IN THE WORLD

By Linda Hayward

Illustrated by
Joe Ewers

A Step 1 Book

Random House/
Children's Television Workshop

Some butter.

Some sugar.

Some eggs.

Some flour.

Some chocolate chips.

What time is it, Cookie Monster?

Time to make cookies!

Time to mix.

Time to roll.

Time to bake.

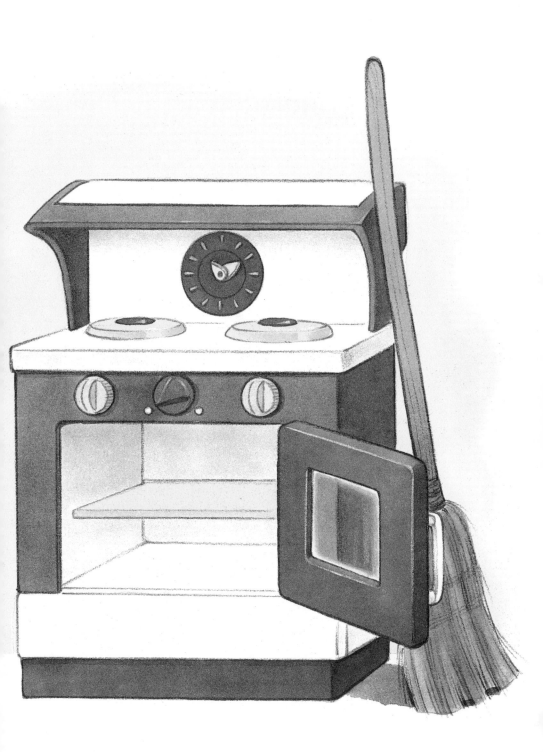

Dum-de-dum.

Time to wait.

Time to think about
the BIGGEST cookie
in the world!

Some butter.

Some sugar.

Some eggs.

Some flour.

Some chocolate chips.

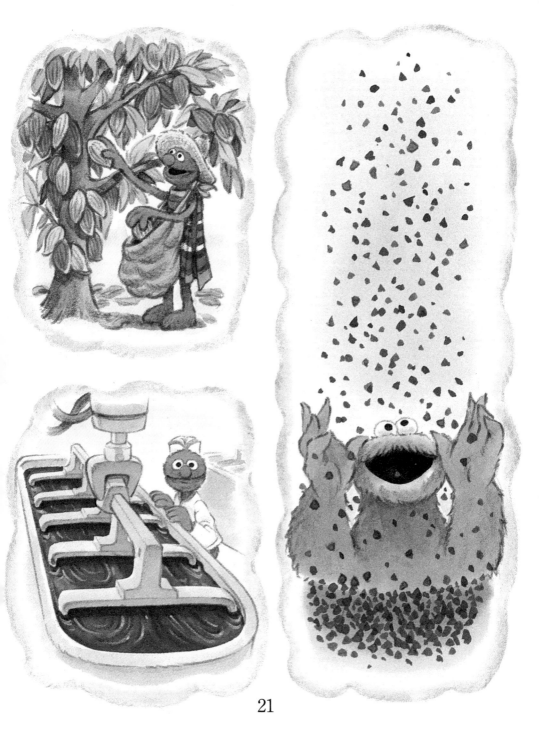

Time to mix.

Time to roll.

Time to bake.

Cowabunga!
Time to eat!

Uh-oh.

Something is burning.

Time to start over.

Some butter.

Some sugar.

Some eggs.

Some flour.

Some chocolate chips....